Hope

When All Else Fails

Takudzwa Shumba

Trafford PUBLISHING®   www.trafford.com
North America & international
toll-free: 1 888 232 4444 (USA & Canada)
fax: 812 355 4082

This book is dedicated to my family; thank you for being there for me at my worst and best. Mum and dad in honor of your memory I dedicate this book and most importantly, to GOD, I couldn't have done anything without your grace and favor upon me. Thank you.

Prologue

Walking down the driveway on a beautiful night, a man, a woman and a little boy enjoy a fresh breeze of air.

Woman: What would you like to become when you grow up Joshua?

Joshua: Mummy I want to sing and preach in church.

Man: That's my boy. Why sing and preach?

Joshua: When I sing people will cry and receive Jesus and when I preach they will learn about Him.

Man: Who taught you that?

Joshua: Aunt Helen at church. I like church. We pray, we sing and we learn about Jesus.

Woman: Yes Joshua and only good boys who listen to God and His word will get closer to Him.

Joshua: Yes mu . . . . (*There is a sudden bang and a car rushing towards Joshua. The man pushes Joshua out of harm's way* *and he is run over instead. The car continues out of control lifting the woman into the air finally crashing unto a nearby tree*.) Dad? *(Crying)* Dad stand up please!!!!!!!!

Man: *(Faintly gasping for air with tears in his eyes)* . . . . I . . . . Lo.lo.love you son

Chapter One

Joshua: April we cannot keep up like this.

April: Like what if I may ask?

Joshua: Like strangers. I am trying my best to get your dad to like me. I am not wild the way he says I am. It's just that a lot has been going on lately. My mom hasn't been well since dad had the hospital scare. I got Chad and Drew to protect as well.

April: You got a son and a daughter. I have tried my best to cover for you but I can't anymore. My dad is the church Bishop; I'm an unwed mother of two at 22 years of age with an undecided fiancé who is not committed to settling down. What do you want me to do? I've humiliated my family enough don't you think?

Joshua: Look I'm sorry, I'm trying okay. At the moment I'm just trying that's all I can do. (**_Someone enters the room_**)

Victoria: Oh my . . . . I'm sorry did I interrupt something?

Joshua: No mom it's okay we were just leaving.

Victoria: Don't leave on my account.

April: Thank you Mrs Jones but we were leaving.

Victoria: Okay dear. Greet your parents for me. Bless you dear. Josh pick up your father's letters at the office for me.

Joshua: Sure thing mom. Let's go April . . . *(They leave)*

MEANWHILE . . .

Tina: Abel what's wrong?

Abel: I don't know. I've been having a weird dream lately. I see a young man without anything crying hopelessly. When I get closer to him, he drifts away. I try talking to him and all he says is he's sorry he killed his dad. I've been praying lately and my spirit keeps leading me to pray for this young man. He's troubled Tina. I don't know what that has got to do with me but we will wait on the Lord.

Tina: I know it's confusing but the Lord knows and He will provide the answer.

Abel: I know my dear; it just seems a burden too big but no need to worry. I got to go to work and I will pass by the church for a few minutes to drop the minute book.

Tina: Okay dear. I will see you later.

Sally: April your father is the church Bishop of hundreds of people and I'm his wife. For how long will you embarrass us? What are people going to say?

April: For once can you be just my mum and dad. I got pregnant to get your attention but it doesn't seem to have worked.

Sally: Do you know we've worked so hard to be where we are and we can't afford to have your childish tantrums mess it up. You know how we feel about that boy. We will take care of your children. That boy has issues. You need to stay away from him.

April: Oh like you did with me. Spend all my years in the hands of church members so you can build your church. No thank you very much. I want love for my children and I will give them that believe me. If you wanted to build your church so much you shouldn't have had me and I thought judging was for God. You do not know Josh and you do not even try to know him. He is my fiancé and my children's dad. For goodness sake I've got enough problems mother.

Sally: I am not having this conversation again April Anders. You will talk to your father next time maybe he will put some sense in you.

April: He could try and we will see . . . . (*A little boy runs in*) Jojo

Jojo: Hi mummy! Where is dad?

April: He is outside waiting for us.

Jojo: Bye Nana (***Running outside***)

Sally: Bye Jo. Please minimise the family embarrassment and be home early with the kids.

April: Whatever appeases you mother. (***She leaves and her phone rings***); Joey?

Joey: Hi! You didn't reply my messages

April: There wasn't anything to reply to.

Joey: I actually do care April. I want to be a part of you and your kids. They like me and I do like them too. I go to church, I serve the Lord and your dad really likes me and I respect him. What more do you want?

April: Look I do respect you and all that but I'm sorry I don't need anyone new in my life at the moment. I got to go and please stop calling or texting. I'm sorry but just stop. (***She hangs up and gets in the car***)

Joshua: Everything alright?

April: Yes. Just need some fresh air.

Joshua: Me too.

Peter: I cannot die without telling him the truth Victoria. I killed his father and mother. I have lived with that for 21years. I want to die in peace.

Victoria: He should know you are not his father. I agree with you.

Peter: Your father dies saving your life and your mother is lifted off the ground into the air and crashes to her death when you are just 5 years old and you see these things right before your eyes. You suppress those memories and they become just nightmares so you can move on. I'm the father he knows but justice needs to be done.

Victoria: You overcompensate for it by rejecting your sons.

Peter: I didn't do such a thing. I have loved the 3 of them equally. Both of us know you aren't his super fan.

Victoria: I admit it. Joshua isn't my flesh; he is your charity case. He doesn't deserve a dime of that wealth and I will make sure he doesn't get it.

Peter: It was never about the money Vicky. It's about what I owe that boy I left in the driveway 21 years ago.

Victoria: I don't care what you think you owe him. I just want my boys to get their father's love they miss and deserve not some stranger orphan.

Peter: One day you will know what I'm talking about Vicky. If I die I pray the Lord changes your heart because if anything happens to that boy due to your hatred towards him you shall never find peace. Remember this conversation Vicky. As much as I love you, God's will comes first.

Victoria: I'm a Christian remember.

Peter: You are a church goer, people pleaser and know it all religious individual. There is a difference.

Victoria: How dare you say spiteful things about your wife Peter Jones?

Peter: Because it's the truth. When you are dying Vicky your life flashes before your eyes and there are things which happen which are inexplicable. When the time comes you will understand . . . . *(Joshua enters the room with April and the kids)*

Jojo: Papi . . . .

Peter: Oh my boy! Come here.

Joshua: Mom, they send the letters home.

Victoria: Okay I will check the mail when I get home. I was just leaving.

Joshua: Alright mom. Hi dad! How have you been?

Peter: Breathing. Could I have a word? *(April leaves)* This is hard for me but I got to say this. Joshua I'm not your father.

Chapter Two

Joshua sits down in shock.

Peter: 21 years ago I had a fight with Victoria. I left the home so angry I went for a drink at the bar. I thought I was just going to clear my head but I ended up drinking like a fish. I sat behind the wheel and on my way home; a car flashed its light in my eyes . . . . *(He breathes for a while)*I lost control of the car. Your dad, you and your mum were walking on the driveway. My car was headed for you but your dad pushed you out of the way and I hit him instead. I turned the steering and I lift your mum off the ground. Those nightmares you had were not nightmares but the events that occurred the night I . . . . killed your parents. I am dying but I could not die without telling you the truth. I am not at peace. Every night I go . . . . *(Joshua interrupts)*

Joshua: Just stop . . . . Please just stop. *(Looking confused)* I just need a moment.

Peter: I know. I wish I could turn back the clock. Things are going to get tough for you but remember these words; "God has a greater plan for you so don't lose hope when things fail.

That's the only thing that will get you through." Forgive me Joshua. I am so sorry son. (*He cries*) I never meant to hurt you.

Joshua: It's ok dad. You are my dad it doesn't matter. I love you and I always will. *(Wiping Peter's tears away)* You loved me like your own dad.

Peter: Thank you. *(Tears rolling down his face)* I go in peace son. I can't fight anymore. The years aren't doing me any favours. Remember never give up even when everything falls apart. I'm a bit tired son, I got to rest.

Joshua: Bye dad.

Peter: Bye son. I'm proud of you.

AT CHURCH

Bishop Anders: We come in this place every Sunday as it is a sanctuary for the lost and a healing place for the sick and broken. We do not stand by and watch our brothers and sisters fall into the fires of the enemy. Our God send us here to advice and guide our children into making the right decisions. We do not approve of the ungodly taking advantage of our children. Young people look closer to home. There are young men in this congregation waiting for your hand in marriage.

Congregation: Amen *(People standing up and shouting out)*

Woman: Preach on bishop

Bishop Anders: Okay sit down, sit down. God forgives us for making mistakes but we can't keep making the same mistakes over and over again on the basis that God forgives us. We need to change brothers and sisters. We need a new spirit, a new hunger, a new perspective and a new fire for God to take us to greater heights. I want to get there and I don't want to go alone. Shift brothers and sisters. Shift, shift and keep on shifting. The Lord is waiting for you. He can't do this alone. He wants you to go with Him. Come on. *(He speaks in tongues as the congregation makes noise)* Where are you hiding? He is waiting and waiting. Don't make Him wait any longer. Go move with Him. Let Him carry you when you can't move anymore. Many of you wonder why I preach like this, I will tell you. You know I've got two wonderful grandkids. When my daughter fell pregnant, I didn't move with God. I was ashamed and angry at her as any father would if your daughter has a full life ahead of them and suddenly tells you they have to put those plans on hold because they are pregnant. You want to curse the man who did that to her but God asked me a few questions; did you sit down and advise her of the world? Did you spend enough time with her to teach her about how deceiving the devil can be? You did not fulfil your duties so why are you angry at her? It got me thinking and I realised it's never too late with God. I amnow fulfilling my duties. Fulfil yours and move with Him.*(People start standing up and shouting out)* I am leaving it here and will continue next Sunday. Don't miss out people of God, move when He moves and your life will never be the same again. God bless you all. Have a blessed week in Jesus' name. *(He walks off the pulpit)*

Congregation: Amen *(Shouting and clapping in excitement continues)*

As Bishop Anders walks off the stage, Joey, the youth leader approaches him.

Bishop Anders: Joey! How are you doing?

Joey: Bishop, I'm alright sir. I've got some bad news. Mr Peter Jones passed away a couple of hours ago. His wife was on the way to church when she received the news so she is now at home with a few mourners. I was going to join them on my way home.

Bishop Anders: Thank you son. I need to get my wife first and hope to meet you there.

Joey: No problem sir. *(He leaves and so does the bishop)*

AT JONES RESIDENCY

Woman: Oh my dear Victoria, be strong in the Lord and your grief shall not take over your life. Peter was a great man and he is with the Almighty now.

Victoria: Thank you

Man: *(Approaching from behind)* I'm sorry for your loss ma'am

Victoria: Thank . . . . *(Looking behind)* Russell! What are you doing here? I said after the funeral so we could tell the boys.

I need to be the grieving widow not a lustful lover looking at her love across the room. We don't want to raise eyebrows.

Russell: We won't. I'm sorry just couldn't stay away I miss you very much.

Joshua approaches Victoria

Joshua: Mum I got to . . . . oh I'm sorry for interrupting. I didn't know . . . .

Russell: It's okay young man. I'm sorry for your loss

Joshua: Me too sir. Me too. If I didn't know I would pass you for Drew and Chad's dad.

Russell: They are family. I'm Peter's young brother. Despite being estranged I loved him though he never forgave me. I tried to make it right but he never gave me a second of his day. He was my big brother after all that's why I came.

Joshua: I saw you at the hospital the day before last

Russell: He didn't give me a chance to talk but I left him a message that I was sorry and I forgive him. I pray his soul rests in peace.

Joshua: Too bad we meet under such circumstances anyway since you are family I will say whatever I came to say. Mum I got a call from After Life Funeral Directors. They said dad arranged everything before he died and he gave them my details and spoke to the hospital so if it's okay I'm going to go and talk to them and sort out the documents for his burial.

Victoria: Alright Joshua . . . . *(He leaves)*

Russell: He seems like a nice young man. What have you got against him?

Victoria: Despite him not being my son, I do not do charity cases. You know me better than that Rus.

Russell: Yes I do know you more than anyone needs to know . . . . *(A woman approaches)*

Woman: Ooooh Vicky I didn't know *(embracing her)*. He was a very good man. Only a few can measure up to him. I pray his soul found peace at the end.

Victoria: Thank you very much

Woman: No problem my dear. We are here for you after all. We all need friends, family and even strangers to grieve with us at one point in life. I will leave you darling for work but I'm going to meet you at the funeral tomorrow. Take good care of your family my dear. *(She leaves)*

Russell: I can't stay for long Vicky. The least I could do is honour Pete by leaving but I will be back tomorrow.

FUNERAL DAY AT CHURCH

Bishop Anders: We always meet, smile, say goodbye and hope to see each other the next day but sometimes when we part, we forget that it might be the last we will be smiling at each other . . . . Lying here is a great man with a great heart but that is all gone except his legacy. This is a difficult time for everyone but lest we forget it's a time to celebrate Mr Peter Jones, a loving husband, father, brother, grandfather and friend. A man of great integrity, who gave his all to serve the Almighty God, a man who believed that a simple act of love can cancel hatred between enemies, a man who taught me that God does not look for perfect people and above all, a man who showed me that being human is all you can ever be on this earth because if you become spirit your realm needs to change as well. I would like to leave this opportunity to the family. *(He sits down as Joshua steps onto the stage)*

Joshua: Good morning everyone! Thank you Bishop for giving me this opportunity. I am . . . . I . . . . (*He looks down on the paper he is holding and crumbles it. He puts it in his pocket*) I had written down what I wanted to say but it feels empty . . . . Well, (*He sighs*), the man lying down in that casket called me to visit him in the hospital the day before he passed. He told me the news every child doesn't ever wish to hear. He told me that I am not his biological son . . . . (*There is total silence in the room*) . . . . I'm an orphaned boy who had and still has nightmares from witnessing his parents killed right before his eyes by this man. He cried as he told me that for the past 21years he had been trying to pay the price for what he did. I wanted to walk out, to curse him but you know I said something totally different, I said, "It doesn't matter, you are my dad and will always be." He cried even more and I asked myself why I couldn't hate this man who took away my real family from me and I felt a feeling which I could only deduce to be love. It was love that my dad had in him that made him take me as his own instead of running away like most hit and runs offenders do. Every decision I made he never criticised me for it, he let me make mistakes and learn from them. With Chad and Drew looking up to me he told me it's my choice as a big brother to mould them or destroy them. To me Peter Jones wasn't a man who just took me in out of guilt or a dad who paid tuition fees and let me do whatever I want, he was a mentor, a role model, a great friend but most of all the best father and husband you could find on this earth. His love for mom, Chad, Drew and I will forever remain a part of us. I am not saddened by these events but humbled by his departure as I've learnt how he was a key to uncovering the destinies of more than half of the people in this room. All I can say to him is, "Dad we've lost a legend but God has gained a child. We might be in sorrow over your departure but at least we had years with you. Your big heart and great generosity will forever be a path of example for us. Keep smiling and we smile as well. Even though I'msaying goodbye it's not because it's the end but because you can go and start ahead before we follow. You will foreverbe loved and missed." Goodbye dad. *(**He leaves the stage**)*

Bishop Anders: I believe we could all rise up and pay our respect to Mr Jones as we progress to our next venue.

People progress to the burial site as they pay their last respects as he is laid to rest. As people disperse Joshua remains standing looking over the grave site holding his son's hand.

Jojo: Dad is Papi gone to heaven?

Joshua: Yes Jojo, Papi's gone to heaven.

Jojo: Will we ever see him again?

Joshua: If we are good boys and girls, God will take us to him.

Jojo: Is it okay to miss him because I miss him already.

Joshua: It's more than okay to miss him. I think Papi would like that but we should not be sad when we miss him. *(A man approaches)*

Man: Excuse me Mr Jones. My name is Abel Thunders, I knew both of your real parents and Peter. Give me a call sometime and we can talk. *(He hands him his card)* I'm sorry for your loss. God is with you. *(He leaves)*

Jojo: Who is that man daddy?

Joshua: I don't know son but we better get going people will be waiting for us. *(He places the card in his coat)*

Chapter Three

Lawyer: Thank you all for coming. Mr Russell Jones I thank you for your presence as it was your brother's request that I contact you at this time.

Russell: As surprised as I am, I'm happy to be here as well

Lawyer: Now then, shall we?

Joshua: Yes, go ahead

Lawyer: Thank you. *(He takes out the will and starts reading),* I Peter Jones leave this will behind as my final role as a father and husband. I built an empire I leave today for my family. I was a man of great pride but as I've learnt, pride goes before a fall. Wealth never brought me happiness for a moment in my entire life. I have loved from the heart but in return have been loved for money. I make this will short to save everyone from boredom. Chad and Drew I leave 30% each of the value of my wealth and the remaining 40% I leave it to Josh. There will be grasps in the room especially from my wife but as per my wishes, I leave my empire to Joshua for him to do what he sees fit.

Victoria: What? This is ridiculous. I'm leaving

Joshua: Wait. *(Victoria halts)* Pardon me sir. I do not want anything. I just want to take care of my brothers if I may sign a document to give it all to mum.

Victoria: Yes can he do that? *(Getting closer to the lawyer)*

Lawyer: It's funny you know because Peter said that's what's going to happen and he made me draft those documents. So yes you can but after I finish reading.

Victoria: Then get on because we do not have time to waste. *(She sits down)*

Lawyer: I shall continue . . . . To my young brother Russell, I had you called that you may witness the real meaning of love. You may not understand now but one day you will. To Victoria I say thank you for making me realise only God can heal the cureless. I truly loved you Vicky. I pray you realise that one day. These are my words as I leave this world . . . . *(Putting the will away)* If I may, in the presence of the people in this room Mr Joshua Jones surrenders all the rights to his wealth to Mrs Victoria Jones from the moment he signs these documents giving him no power or say in the way the company is run. Do you agree?

Joshua: I do

Lawyer: Sign these documents for me sir. *(Joshua signs the documents)* Thank you all for your time. Hope to see you soon. I shall take my leave *(He leaves)*.

Russell: You are a good young man. I admire your nature (*holding Joshua's hand*).

Joshua: Some things are hard to explain sir but are the right things to do. I'm going to leave I need to see my kids.

Russell: No problem son. They are lucky to have you for a dad.

Chad: Can we come with you Josh?

Joshua: Yeah sure

Chad: Cool. I will bring the coats. (*He walks out of the room*)

Drew: (*Shouting after Chad*) and my phone please. See you later mom and Uncle Russell (*Josh and Drew leave*)

Russell: He is a good boy Victoria. You should say thank you.

Victoria: For what? It was mine in the first place.

Russell: No it wasn't. It is rightfully his. Peter did not owe you anything especially afterwhat we did to him. We killed that boy's parents.

Victoria: I'm not listening anymore. I didn't kill anyone. I love you Russell but that don't mean I can't get rid of you.

Russell: No you won't and you know that yourself. I'm those boys' father and you need me especially now. We need to tell them so I will rightfully claim you (*moving closer to Victoria and kissing her ear*) because I'm yearning for you.

Victoria: Rus stop please *(Russell keeps kissing her all over her neck and ears)*. The boys might come back.

Russell: *(not stopping and ripping her top apart)* No they are gone . . . . *(He takes off the rest of her clothes and his)*.

Tina: You have been smiling eversince you came back from Peter's funeral over a week ago. What's going on?

Abel: I met him dear. The boy I have been dreaming about. Do you know the Rivers' son?

Tina: You mean the poor young boy who was orphaned when Peter ran his parents over?

Abel: He is not a boy anymore dear. He a strong, handsome young man and he's got two kids. Peter is the one who adopted him after the incident and he told him on his death bed that he killed his parents.

Tina: Oh my! How did you know all this?

Abel: He spoke at the funeral and said so himself. When he talked something about nightmares I just knew then and there he was the one. I told him I knew both his birth parents and Peter and gave him my card.

Tina: I can't believe this. Praise God my dear. Let's hope he calls soon. When he calls, invite him for dinner and I will tell Keith. They might remember that they were best friends singing at church together.

Abel: Calm down dear. We take one step at a time. We don't rush God.

Tina: I know dear. I'm just so happy I think I will bake some muffins and cake.

Abel: Go ahead dear. That will be good for you

Tina: Keith called earlier. He's bringing his family on Sunday for dinner.

Abel: No problem. I will be in the lounge

AT THE PARK

Jojo: Uncle carry me. I am tired.

Drew: Alright let's play hide and seek. You go and hide and I will look for you. I am counting up to ten. One . . . . *(Jojo shouts)*

Jojo: Wait Uncle I need to run first . . . . *(He runs and shouts)* okay I'm ready

Chad: I'm going to take Karen see the ducks

Joshua: Alright. We will be sat at the bench *(they sit on the park bench)*

April: How are they coping?

Joshua: At nineteen they've lost the man they loved the most . . . . I don't know really. They don't talk about it but they are always clinging to me. Wherever I'm going they want to come too. I guess they are scared of losing me too. I got to re-assure them every time that I'm not going anywhere.

April: I can imagine.

Joshua: I wanted to talk to you about something

April: I'm listening

Joshua: You are not going to like it but can we postpone the wedding?

April: *(loudly)* what????? . . . . You were right, I don't like it. No way am I agreeing to this.

Joshua: It's just that the twins need me more and mum and the company. It's . . . .

April: Stop just stop Josh. What about me, what about your kids? Don't you think we need you as well? Your son lost his Papi; don't you think he needs his dad now? I am tired of waking up in the middle of the night crying without anyone to comfort me. Instead of calling you I need a husband, my children's father to be there for me. (*Now crying*) Josh I am tired of all of it. Why am I the only one sacrificing for our love if there is any to begin with? You can't even tell me how you really feel. No Josh, I am not postponing the wedding. You choose right now, your kids and I or your brothers and mum.

Joshua: April that's not what I meant and you can't expect me to choose.

April: *(Taking off the engagement ring)* When you have decided you know where to find me. *(Almost walking away Josh grabs her hand and stands up to face her)*

Joshua: I'm sorry. I choose you and the kids. You mean more to me. *(Putting back the ring)* No postponing the wedding. We will get married. *(Wiping off her tears)* Don't cry it crushes me. I care so much for you and the kids, I shouldn't have hurt you. I'm sorry babe. Tonight we go out and sleep in the hotel with the kids. Okay?

April: Okay.

AT CHURCH OFFICE

Bishop Anders: Victoria how are you doing?

Victoria: I'm fine Trent

Bishop Anders: How did it go?

Victoria: He signed it over to me in front of the lawyer and all.

Bishop Anders: Everything according to plan?

Victoria: Of course. He won't know what hit him.

Bishop Anders: Perfect. So you now need to make him work more to strain his relationship with my daughter whilst I bring Joey in the picture

Victoria: No problem and my deal is I get to be women's leader

Bishop Anders: That's sorted out already and you sign for all the funds

Victoria: That's more like it. Stay in touch Trent. My regards to Sally

Bishop Anders: You take care of yourself Vicky.

Bishop Anders: April how is it going with that young man?

April: Excuse me?

Bishop Anders: I know I won't get dad of the decade award but I've decided to change all that. I want to support you in all your decisions. So starting now tell me all that's been going on in your life.

April: I don't know what has gotten into you dad but I think I'm going to like this new dad.

Sally: (*Bringing in dinner*) me too.

Jojo: Nana can I have chicken please?

Sally: Okay my little pea (*April's phone rings*)

April: Excuse me it's him

Bishop Anders: Invite him in. Let him join us.

April: (*Surprised*) Dad?

Bishop Anders: Go on. (*She answers*)

April: Yeah . . . . Come in. dad wants you to join us for dinner . . . . Alright. (*She hangs up*)

Bishop Anders: I will usher him in. (*He goes to the door*)

April: Mum?

Sally: I don't know my dear. He came from his office smiling like I've never seen before. Maybe he had an encounter with God. What can we say?

Bishop Anders: Don't be surprised young man. (*Leading him into the dining room*) I haven't been fair to you. I know you wanted to take my daughter and grandkids out for dinner but come join us today and you will take them out another day.

Joshua: Okay sir. (*Pulls a chair out and sits next to April*)

Bishop Anders: Why won't you bless our table son?

Joshua: (*Looks at April first and she nods her head*) okay. Let us pray . . . . Father we thank you for the food on our tables. Bless the hands that made the preparation and the mouths that will feed on it. AMEN. (*People start serving and eat*)

Bishop Anders: So Joshua you holding out alright?

Joshua: Yes sir thank you

Bishop Anders: you planning to take my daughter's hand in marriage

April: Mum?

Sally: Trent?

Bishop Anders: Just making small talk

Joshua: It's alright. Yes sir I do. I plan to make her the happiest woman on earth.

Bishop Anders: That's good. Do you go to church?

Joshua: Yes sir but not recently. Was trying to get things back on track but I do go to church.

Bishop Anders: You know your purpose in life

Joshua: No I don't sir. I believe when I'm ready God will make it plain for me.

Bishop Anders: You are about 26 years old, yes?

Joshua: Yes sir I am 26 years old and yes I got a plan. I'm not lazy I will take care of your daughter and will never hurt her intentionally. I got 2 kids and I'm responsible and with God by my side I will make it. I might not go to church every Sunday but I know there is God and I believe in Him. Are you satisfied? Thank you ma'am the food was nice but I think I will leave

Sally: Stay son it's alright, please? Trent honey come with me to the kitchen please. Thank you (***Trent & Sally go to the kitchen***)

April: You okay?

Joshua: Yeah I guess so. Your dad . . . . (***She interrupts***)

April: I know. He is showing interest but he got a force of habit. I'm sorry

Joshua: I can't sleep here though (*Jojo interrupts*)

Jojo: Dad today you will tuck me in.

Joshua: Okay little man but you have to finish your chicken first

Jojo: But . . . .

Joshua: What did I tell you before?

Jojo: No buts when you are eating. Everyone must finish off their food

Joshua: Otherwise . . . .

Jojo: No games

Joshua: That's my boy. Finish off and I will tuck you in. Karen sleeping?

April: Yeah. Can't go hotel today maybe another time?

Joshua: Sure . . . .

Chapter Four

Joshua: How can my employment be terminated Lawrence?

Lawrence: I wish I knew Josh. I was as surprised as you are but those were the orders.

Joshua: From whom?

Lawrence: Your mum. I am sorry man. I don't want to do this but it's either you or me and I got a family to feed.

Joshua: It's alright. Thanks man. I will go and see her. See you later

---

AT HOME

Victoria: (*Lying in bed naked with Russell*) Finally I get all I want. Josh fired and I will make his life miserable that he may leave.

Russell: What are you talking about?

Victoria: Nothing

Russell: Vicky you can't say nothing. This hatred thing is getting out of hand. That boy does nothing but love you. You do not do charity cases but I think you are making a big mistake. Is that the reason why you overworked him to get him fired from the job? He won't have anything left. He confided in me a couple of days ago that he was having problems with April because he has been working endlessly he hasn't seen his kids in almost 3 weeks. (***Victoria smiles***) why are you smiling? Don't tell me you had something to do with this as well? Jesus Christ!

Victoria: If you feel pity for him go with him then. I don't need either of you

Russell: that's where you are wrong. You need me and I don't need to explain myself. (***Joshua shouts from downstairs***)

Joshua: Mum, mum, mum, mum?

Russell: You got some explaining to do (***Footsteps approaching the bedroom and the door opens***)

Victoria: Can't you knock?

Joshua: I'm sorry; I didn't think I would find you in bed in the stroke of midday.

Victoria: Now you found me get out.

Joshua: (***Agitated***) No

Victoria: What?

Joshua: Why was I fired?

Victoria: You are just fired.

Joshua: The past 3 weeks I've overworked and I haven't seen my kids or fiancée . . . . (*She interrupts*)

Victoria: If you have one

Joshua: What's that supposed to mean? Is that what you were trying to do? Break my relationship and get what?

Victoria: So you thought Bishop Anders just decided to show interest in your relationship with his daughter to accommodate you into family. Get this in your head, you don't have family, no one loves you Joshua. You are just a hopeless orphan. Get that in your head and move on.

Joshua: (*Angrily*) Shut up. What did I ever do wrong to you? All I ever did was love you and respect you like my mum but you don't deserve to have any of that. You think I don't know that you never wanted anything to do with me? I knew that the moment I overhead you telling dad that I disgust you and you never loved me. When dad told me I wasn't his or yours I knew that's why you never loved me. Victoria you don't deserve anything you have. I can't live here anymore I'm going.

Victoria: all your accounts have been frozen as well.

Joshua: You are so clever aren't you? You had planned everything. Tell me one thing before I go, when dad killed my parents, why was he drunk?

Victoria: Oh that! Funny story really, he caught me in bed with Russell and I told him I had always loved Russell and that I was pregnant with Russell's twins. He was so devastated according to him that he tried to drink the pain away. The next thing I know was I became your mother because you had severe trauma that you didn't even know who you were or your parents. You started having those nightmares but Peter said we shouldn't tell you what had happened.

Joshua: One thing I will tell you is what goes around comes back around. Watch your back Victoria because when it comes back for you it will hurt more than mine.

Drew: (*Enters the bedroom*) you can't leave Josh. We heard everything.

Joshua: I'm sorry kid but I got to. At least your real dad is here for you now. I got none of that anymore. I need to go and tell April how I feel and see my kids.

Victoria: Leave the keys to the car. Just take what you are wearing because all belongs to me.

Chad: Mum how could you?

Victoria: Young man I'm your mother you do not talk to me like that. Russell is your real dad. Get to know him.

Russell: Josh . . . (*Josh looks at him*) I'm sorry for everything

Joshua: I know. (*He leaves*)

Russell: I'm sorry kids you got to find out like this.

Drew: It's alright dad told us before he died but he made us promise not to say a word but I guess now we can say it.

Russell: Guess you hate me right now

Chad: No dad said it wasn't your fault. He stopped you from coming so we wouldn't be confused at a young age. We cool with it but we will always love him more hope you understand that.

Russell: No problem. You want to go anywhere or do something together.

Drew: I think if you could get us Josh back first that would be good. You may not understand but we love him

Russell: I know how you feel I'm a little brother as well but sometimes it's good to give big brothers some space. They will be in touch when they are ready

Victoria: Oh please! Don't you have something better to talk about and you two aren't you supposed to be at school?

Chad: Got back for lunch

Victoria: Have your lunch then and go back.

Russell: Call me and I will drive you back

Chad: Alright.

Joey: How was it?

April: Joey no after sex talk. We shouldn't have done this in the first place. How did we get in my bed at midday and have sex?

Joey: You called me crying about your fights with Josh. I came over and we sat in your room. You just talked whilst I listened and you kissed me and you know what happened afterwards.

April: Oh my God! (*Covering her face*)

Joey: Hey! Look at me, (*She looks at him*), you are a very beautiful woman who deserves happiness. I can give you that. I love you so much April that every night I pray that you love me the way I love you I . . . . (*April's door opens*)

Sally: I tried stopping him. (*Josh just stood there speechless and turned around to leave*)

Joshua: Where is my son and daughter?

Sally: Josh?

Joshua: Ma'am please. I don't know if you have had a day like the one I had. I just want to die at the moment so please get me my son and daughter. I want to see them and I will leave never to bother you again. I will be sat in your kitchen. Thank you (*He goes downstairs*)

April: Get dressed please and leave

Joey: April?

April: Just get dressed alright

Jojo: (*Running in the kitchen*) Daddy . . . . (*He throws himself into his arms*). I miss you daddy why didn't you come and see me?

Joshua: I am here now son. I missed you too a lot.

Sally: Have something to drink son.

Joshua: No thank you ma'am (*He puts Jojo on one lap and Karen on another*). Thank you for bringing me my kids ma'am I really appreciate it.

April: (*Entering the kitchen*) Josh?

Joshua: (*He ignores her*) Jojo, dad is going away for a while okay. I won't see you in a long time but I will come back for you.

Jojo: But dad . . . .

Joshua: (*Interrupting*) it's alright son. I need to find a new job and a new home and build you all those things you wanted. Uncle Drew and Chad will come see you for me okay. Take care of Karen.

Karen: Dada . . . . (*Everyone looks at her*)

Joshua: You said your first word . . . . Oh God. I love you sweetie, both of you very much. Look out for each other. Ma'am thank you. I'm going. (*He hugs and kisses his kids and leave. April follows him*)

April: Josh please talk to me (*He stops and looks at her*)

Joshua: What? There is nothing to talk about. I have had the worst day of my entire life. I lost my job because my mum had me fired. She overworked me to fight with you. I came to make things right and surprise I got quite the package of disappointments and betrayals today.

April: That's not it and you know it.

Joshua: No I don't know. My fiancée is sleeping with another man for comfort because we've been fighting. I do not sleep around because I have fought with you. Who are you? What have you done to April? I don't want this whore . . . . (*She slaps him hard whilst crying*)

April: I am not a whore and you don't have the right to call me that. I don't know you either Josh. You don't tell me anything. You are just a coward

Joshua: Wow you just hit me and you are now calling me a coward. Now listen to me, I have told you all that was going on with my family and I mean everything but I know what you want to hear April. I came here to resolve our problems and tell you what I really felt and I will still say it before I leave because it has lost its value I guess.

April: don't . . . . (*He interrupts*)

Joshua: (*He breathes deeply and waits a moment before speaking*) I love you April Anders but it's no good now is it? I love you so much that right now I feel so betrayed and angry that I just want to cry. (*Tears fall from his eyes*) this is the first time I have cried in 21years but it feels right. I am hurting so much that I don't want to talk anymore. I feel like my life has been a façade and I have never had an identity. I have always been invisible. I don't want to live anymore; I just want to be re-born and never meet anyone from Victoria to you. Right now I hate myself more than I hate anything else. I have always loved you. I never said it because I was afraid if I say it I lose you. Right now I have said it and I have lost you. All I have now is just me. Please when our kids ask where daddy is tell them he will be back. I don't want to talk to you or see you ever again April. My love for you has just been clouded by anger. I don't know if it's strong enough to resurface. (*She gets closer to him*)

April: (*Crying*) Josh I'm sorry (*She hugs him*)

Joshua: Tell your dad he has won. (*He kisses her for one last time*) I have to go (*He starts walking away and Joey comes out and embraces April as she cries uncontrollably*)

Jojo: (*Running towards Josh*) daddy wait . . . (*Josh stops and looks around*)

Joshua: I got to go son.

Jojo: Can I come with you then?

Joshua: You got school little man. We can't allow you to miss it. I will come back for you I promise

Jojo: That's what you said last time but didn't come back for ages.

Joshua: This time I mean it (*He hugs him*) I love you little man. Now go to nana and I will see you soon okay?

Jojo: Okay. Next time bring some new toys dad because the ones I have are too old.

Joshua: I got it. Go on now. (*Jojo runs back as Josh wipes off the tears from his eyes and speaks to himself*) Get it together Josh. (*He walks away without looking back*).

Chapter Five

Joshua: Excuse me! How much is the bread?

Shopkeeper: That will be a pound.

Joshua: I only got 95pence can't I get something else. (*The shopkeeper looks at him for a moment*)

Shopkeeper: You know what; get the bread and a bottle of cola for free. Keep your change okay?

Joshua: Thank you sir. (*He gets the bread and cola and leaves. As he walks through the streets he sees an old lady on a bus stop asking for change from passers. He approaches her and sits next to her*). Are you hungry ma'am? We could share some of my bread. (*The old lady is hesitant*) Don't worry I'm just helping. My name is Joshua

Old Lady: (*Taking the bread*) thank you young man. I'm Rose.

Joshua: Nice to meet you Rose. I will call you Mama Rose. You are a very beautiful young lady.

Rose: *(Blushing)* Oh don't flatter me young man. Are you from here?

Joshua: I'm from everywhere. Wherever I fall asleep is my home.

Rose: A young handsome man like you shouldn't be on the street.

Joshua: Oh the streets don't have a type. Anyone can be on them and they will give everyone a home that needs one.

Rose: Fair point. I like you; do you have anywhere to sleep?

Joshua: No I don't. Will you share your presidential suite with me?

Rose: *(Laughing)* Yes I will. It would be an honour Mr Vice President.

Joshua: I like that, a good sense of humour. (***Standing up***) Give me those bags I will carry them.

Rose: Oh son they are a lot son I don't want to hurt you.

Joshua: No it's okay. I need to put these muscles to work. You lead the way and I will follow. *(They start walking slowly to Rose's pace and conversing)* How long have you been here?

Rose: 15years going on 16 and you?

Joshua: 4weeks. Why that long? Have you got no family?

Rose: I do. It's not a story I like to share that often.

Joshua: Will you tell me then? We could start our happy family with our sad life journeys.

Rose: You seem like a very nice boy. I will tell you when we've sat down and eaten.

Joshua: I only got 95pence to my name what can we buy?

Rose: There is a chip shop by the corner from where I live. They will give me lots for 50pence so for 95pence I believe we will get a good portion.

Joshua: That's good news. I could eat a whole bowl of food at the moment. I will save the bread and we have a new guest homecoming party *(Rose laughs)*

Rose: Joshua I'm too old to be laughing like this please.

Joshua: No problem Mama Rose. I will wait till the party.

Bishop Anders: Sally I am not having this conversation with you.

Sally: Excuse me Trent. Sorry for being your wife but I would like to know why I do not have the right to sign off any of our accounts.

Bishop Anders: You are my wife that's all you have to be. I do the signing off of money

Sally: Trent; are you implying that I stole some money?

Bishop Anders: Did you? *(Sally keeps quiet)* Its final Sally I am the head of this house what I say goes

Sally: Since when? Trent all the years we have been married I have supported you and served you and God faithfully. Why all of a sudden are things changing?

Bishop Anders: They just need to change.

Sally: Do you know the embarrassment it caused when I went to the bank to sign off some money and to be taken by security as they thought I was stealing . . . . You know what; arguing with you is hopeless. You have done enough damage as it is. I love you but I'm afraid you are alone now in your decisions Trent. I do not know you anymore. I am going to start cooking . . . . *(Joey walks in)*

Joey: Sorry is this a bad time?

Sally: No son I was leaving . . . come on in *(**Sally goes to the kitchen where April and the kids are**)*

Joey: Sir you wanted to see me

Bishop Anders: Come and take a seat son.

IN THE KITCHEN . . . .

Jojo: Nana is dad coming back today?

Sally: Not yet darling. He said soon

Jojo: I haven't spoken to him or seen him in ages *(**The phone rings**)*

Sally: *(**Picks up the phone**)* . . . . Hello

HOPE

Joshua: Yes ma'am, its Josh

Sally: How are you son?

Joshua: I am fine ma'am. Can I speak to Jojo please?

Sally: hold on son. Jojo your dad wants to speak to you (*Jojo grabs the phone quickly*)

Jojo: Daddy why are you not coming to see us. Karen is saying dada every day and we miss you dad.

Joshua: (*Emotionally*) I know son. I miss you too. I will come soon. I haven't finished work but very soon. Dad is coming soon

Jojo: Leave the work daddy. I just want to see you. Come home daddy please . . . I beg you daddy. (*Now crying*) we can stay without food and toys daddy, we just want you.

Joshua: it's okay Jojo. Daddy is coming home okay. Don't cry anymore. Okay?

Jojo: okay daddy. (*Wiping his tears*) Do you want to speak to mum?

Joshua: No Jojo. Give nana the phone. I love you son

Jojo: I love you too dad. Nana . . . . (*Sally gets the phone*)

Sally: I am here.

Joshua: I am sorry ma'am but I can't call anymore. I don't have anything. I sleep anywhere warm. I had to sacrifice the little

I had to call. Please take care of my kids. I know you will do the right thing. You got a good heart. I'm sorry ma'am. I wish things had been different

Sally: I understand. You take care of yourself out there. I will pray for you. I am sorry for judging you and acting spiteful towards you son. You never deserved it

Joshua: it's okay ma'am. I never held it against you. I got to go. God bless you *(He hangs up)*

Sally: April????????????

April: Nothing mum. I got Joey now. I don't care

Sally: I was wrong about him honey. He is a good man. You need to make this right

April: Nothing about him affects me anymore mum. There is nothing to make right. He is the one who left.

Sally: You sure are your father's daughter. You have both become something I don't know. You hurt him darling. I know he had to sort out his priorities right but when I opened the door to your bedroom that day I thought you would be talking to Joey not sleeping with him honey. I felt his anger and pain. If anything happens to that boy we are all accountable for our actions towards him. From the Jones' house to our house God will punish us.

April: Now you are taking his side.

Sally: I don't take sides anymore. I take God's will. Anyway since you don't care about him, I will look for him alone for Karen and Jojo's sake. They need their dad and since I am the only one who seems to care about him now, I will find him with the Lord's help.

Rose: How do you feel?

Joshua: Angry, hurt, and betrayed?

Rose: By who if I may ask?

Joshua: Everyone especially God.

Rose: That's why you keep that façade son and keep on hurting. God gives you grace son but you can't have it all by grace alone, you need to earn the other blessings in store and position yourself that His favour increases upon your life. God is not man. You do not categorise God with man. You need to sort out yourself first.

Joshua: What do you mean?

Rose: Sit down. I promised to tell you my story and I will tell you now. At least you have looked after me for a week so I believe it's fair I tell you. Almost 15 years ago I was a Pastor's wife and I still am since I didn't divorce anyone. When I first met my husband, he was hungry for God. Everyone laughed at him but I saw a man who loved God so much that I fell in love with him instantly. When he approached me he made it clear that God was his number one priority no matter what. I told him I felt the same. We began seeking the Lord together, encouraging one another. We needed a source of income and we worked tirelessly until we got married. The Lord visited us frequently that we never lacked. Our church was so small when we started but God started bringing people. We were blessed that we build a big church for GOD. Everything was like a fairy-tale and I never stopped seeking the Lord's guidance because I couldn't conceive. I remember praying endlessly but there was never an answer. One day my husband started acting funny. He would not come home and say he was praying at church. I never doubted him. I believed him because I was so blinded by my love. Then things started changing. He would shout at me and hit me. I was in denial but he started involving his younger brother who is also a pastor and his mother. They all ganged up on me that when I fell pregnant they said I had cheated on him. His mother allowed me to stay because she desperately wanted a grandchild. Little did I know that he had twins with the worship leader at church who was a single mother of one which later turned out it was his son already. When I gave birth to my daughter, I never held her in my arms. I was not allowed to be alone with her. When my daughter was about 10 years of age, I told her I was her mother and she screamed at me and she told my husband I had tried to kidnap her. My husband was renting a flat for me so I could see my daughter but after I told my daughter I was her mum my husband made sure I suffer and I was left homeless. I never saw any of them again. For the past years I tried desperately but without success and I gave up on God because things were not happening the way I wanted them to. I hated myself so much I was about to commit suicide when the wind blew on my bible and opened **Revelations 21** and **verse 4** stuck in my heart which says, *"**And God will wipe away every tear from their eyes; there shall be no more**"* *death, nor sorrow, nor crying. There shall be no more pain, for the former things have passed away."* From that day I stopped being angry and went back straight to my knees to do only what has always felt right in my life, which is seeking God earnestly and serving Him in any way I can. Son we all don't deserve what we have but by His grace we got it. It is never God's fault we are in trouble. He gives us grace but we can't have it all by grace alone. He wants intimacy with us. He does not want to share us with anything. If you love Him, love Him whole heartedly.

Joshua: So why are you still on the streets if God is with you? *(With tears in his eyes)*

Rose: There is nothing wrong with being on the streets when God's presence is upon you son. Maybe my destiny is to be here with you. Everything happens for a reason son and it's okay to cry to God son.

Joshua: *(Tears falling down his cheeks)* But you don't understand . . . .

Rose: I may not but God does. Tell me what happened to you?

Joshua: *(Sniffing and wiping away his tears)* When I was five my mother and father were killed in an accident. My dad died saving me. The man who killed my parents adopted me because I was suffering from post-traumatic stress disorder I only remembered the accident as nightmares. When I was growing up his wife never embraced me and one day I overhead her saying telling my dad that I disgust her and she would never love me. I tried to please her but I knew I would never get her affection but I kept on trying so hard but with my dad it was different he loved me so much I never understood. When my dad was dying he told me all about it. He left me 40% of his wealth but I signed it over to mum.

Rose: Do you know what you have Joshua?

Joshua: Suffering, loneliness, pain?

Rose: A good heart and love son. God gave you love because of that good heart. A week ago you offered me bread when you did not have anything and did not even know me son. Not so many people in the streets or even in their homes do that. God wants to use you son.

Joshua: So why did he take everything from me?

Rose: He did not take anything from you. You did that yourself when you tried to buy love from people who love material things. Please God and man who serve truthfully God will be pleased by you. Do you know many are called but few fulfil their purpose earnestly. Many have fallen because they were not satisfied by God's blessings. They want more quickly. They see a business in God's plans for His people. Those people are the ones who will suffer the wrath of God. (***Handing him her bible***) This will help you more than me. I learn of the Lord's word everyday but you need it now before you fall and fail to rise again. Use it wisely

Joshua: But it's yours.

Rose: It's not mine, its God's. It's meant for sharing. I leave you to it. I need some rest dear. (***She gets in her shack as Joshua looks at the bible).***

Chapter Six

Abel: I went looking for Joshua.

Tina: And?

Abel: They do not know where he is.

Tina: What do you mean?

Abel: Apparently he left home. Victoria fired him from the company and they had a fight. He left home to go see his kids and he has not been seen. The little brother told me all this.

Tina: What about calling?

Abel: He called only once almost 8 weeks now since his last call. He told the little brothers to take care of his kids and visit them

Tina: Do you think anything could have happened to him?

Abel: I don't know anymore. We just wait I guess.

Tina: Let's not worry when the time is right he will show up. I had the same dream again.

Abel: About your elder sister?

Tina: Yes but this time she had a young man. She told me it was her son she found on the streets. He had taken care of her and loved her like his own mother.

Abel: I don't know what's happening anymore Tina. It's getting complicated. I pray God makes it clearer. Did you find her husband?

Tina: Yes and he said he doesn't care. She died a long time ago, I should go to the cemetery maybe there is an unknown grave which belongs to her. I wish I hadn't fought with her.

Abel: You were young Tina and you hadn't found the Lord. Don't beat yourself up, pray about it. Maybe she is alive that's why you are dreaming of her now. Don't give up dear. All will be well.

Tina: I will go and make dinner.

Man: Little girl wait up (***Girl increases her pace***) I said wait up ***(He grabs the girl by the hand and tears her top)*** When you asked to wait you stop, okay?

Girl: Please leave me alone. *(Crying)* Please don't do this. I don't want to cause any trouble

Man: Oh aren't you sweet. You have already stirred up trouble where you shouldn't have darling (***He forces his mouth unto hers***)

Joshua: Hey why don't you leave the girl alone? (*The man stops and looks at Joshua*)

Man: My goodness prince charming has arrived. (*Walking toward Josh*)

Joshua: I don't want trouble sir. Could you just leave the girl alone and we all leave peaceful.

Man: I'm sorry but I can't do that because you see I was having a good time here with this lovely lady and you just interrupted my moment. So why don't you back off nicely sir *(poking his chest with sarcasm in his voice)*

Joshua: I'm leaving and with this lady because she doesn't belong to you and you are not going to hurt her.

Man: *(Laughing)* Is that so? (*He punches Josh and they scuffle till Josh is sat on top of the man and keeps punching him until the man cannot fight anymore*)

Joshua: (*walking toward the girl*) What's your name?

Girl: *(Hesitantly)* Grace

Joshua: Okay Grace: you got a lovely name. That man can't hurt you anymore so come with me now okay? *(She resists)* its okay I won't hurt you. I will take you to the bus stop and you go home okay?

Grace: Okay (*She takes his hand*)

Joshua: Good girl. How old are you? Why use this alley?

Grace: 19. I came through here so I can get home quickly my mum is not well so I have to rush home and look after her.

Joshua: It's okay. Next time don't pass by these alleys they are very dangerous especially for young girls like yourself. *(They stop at the bus stop)* Now you go home and take care of your mum.

Grace: *(She hugs Joshua)* thank you for saving me

Joshua: You are most welcome *(She gets on the bus and another man approaches Joshua)*

Man 2: Excuse me sir *(He hands him a handkerchief)* I believe you could use one of this.

Joshua: Thanks *(Sitting down)*

Man 2: No problem. I saw you back in that alley

Joshua: You stalking me now

Man 2: No. it's just that you looked so familiar to my best friend I haven't seen in 21 years.

Joshua: That's a long time not to see a friend don't you think?

Man 2: They say absence makes the heart grow fonder and some friends you never forget especially when they defended you when you were being bullied at church. *(Joshua doesn't respond for a moment and looks at the man's face)*

Joshua: *(Hesitantly)* . . . . Keith Steven Thunders?

Keith: In the flesh . . . . (*He smiles*)

Joshua: Oh my! You clean up nice. I could hug you now but I'm not clean man.

Keith: Does it matter? (*He hugs Josh*) man where did you disappear too?

Joshua: I was here man just relocated to the rich quarters. Married now?

Keith: (*Looks at his ring*) Yes man with two beautiful kids; a 6 year old boy and a 2 year old girl. What about you?

Joshua: Was engaged got a boy and a girl as well; six and one respectively. A long story which I am not too proud to share and just finding my feet at the moment.

Keith: Why worry now? Just come home with me and you will find your feet from there.

Joshua: Appreciate it man but don't hurt the little pride I got left. I'm not alone on these streets. I got an old lady I'm taking care of. I won't leave her here and I got it man. I don't have anything but I believe I will find my feet on these streets.

Keith: (*Extending his business card*) Look man, this is my number. It doesn't matter what time it is just call me when you are ready. I got your back. (*He takes £200 and hands it to him*)

Joshua: No man. I can't.

Keith: I know you will never take it but it's not for you it's for the old lady. You always take care of others Josh and never ask. You got a big heart that only a few possess. God loves you man. Just give Him the worship and exaltation He deserves. Remember we used to sing every opportunity we got and you always made it perfect because you said God is perfect. Trust me if things are tough remember the joy you had in worship. We were full of hope and I believe there still is hope in there somewhere. Don't give up man and don't look at the hurt or disappointments. Please call me when you need anything.

Joshua: Thanks man. Guess we will catch up some time

Keith: I guess so. *(He hugs him again)* I'm so happy to see you man. Everything happens for a reason and at the right season. Remember ***Ecclesiastes 3 verses 1-8*** that should help you. I got to go man

Joshua: I know. It was nice seeing you again (***Keith leaves and Josh speaks to himself***) God do you have to do this to me? *(He walks away)*

Lawrence: I do not know what happened ma'am. The clients said unless they talk to Joshua they are not confirming any deals.

Victoria: Did you tell them he resigned?

Lawrence: I explained it ma'am but they do not care whether he resigned or not, they just want him. They said we bring him back out of resignation or the deals are off. We have only three months to get him or they are done with us.

Victoria: Oh my God! (*Pacing about behind her desk)*

Lawrence: Ma'am you may fire me if you want but I have to say this. What happens in your home is of no concern to me but if it affects the company it becomes my concern. I watched that boy work and interact with other people and all I can say is he is the most polite and trustworthy individual I ever met in my life. He had a brilliant heart full of love and was a respectful fellow. You know why the clients want him? He never promised lies. He gave them the situation as it was. He gave them trust and delivered his promises. To you ma'am; that boy loved you so much even though you hated him. He did all things you asked him, he never questioned you and he defended you when others spoke ill of you. Do you know how many mothers pray for a son like that? When I told him he was fired, I saw hurt and loneliness in his eyes and no rage at all. It was fear of failure I saw that day. I do not know if we find him but I am not looking for him to appease you but for Peter's legacy. God loves him and maybe it was for his best he left but for the company I don't think so. (***He leaves Victoria standing by the window)***

April: Mum what's going on? Why are you crying?

Sally: it's your father.

April: Did something happen to him? What mum? (***Bishop Anders walks** in)*

Bishop Anders: Sally????

Sally: You are as bad as your brother and your mother. How could you do this to me? Trent you are an evil lying cheating bastard.

Bishop Anders: Watch your tone

Sally: Or what? You kick me out like your brother did to Rose.

April: Who is Rose?

Sally: Your uncle's wife. They took away her daughter and made her homeless. No one knows what happened to her. They claimed she had an affair but the child was a splitting image of your uncle. Your cousin disowned her own mother at the age of ten because of your father, uncle and grandmother.

April: Dad is this true?

Bishop Anders: Stay out of it honey

Sally: Why don't you tell your daughter you have been having an affair with Joey's mum and you are his little sister's daddy?

Bishop Anders: Sally please. Leave April out of it

Sally: Why? She is old enough to know her father is a conniving old fool. 15 years having an affair Trent Anders. Was I never good enough for you? Huh?

April: Mum how did you find out? (***Now crying as well***)

Sally: (***Tears still rolling***) I thought I would surprise your father this afternoon for our 25th marriage anniversary. I had prepared his favourite and non-alcoholic bottle of wine and guess what I found. Him and Joey's mum sat on the sofa kissing with little Lorraine showing her dad the reports and the school play she is taking part in. I had to force the truth out of somebody before I ripped out their throat and little Lorraine had some information. She had asked about her dad two years ago and her mum took her to daddy. Trent Anders you have destroyed me (*She cries loudly*)

April: Dad please? Tell me she is lying

Bishop Anders: Honey. It's complicated.

April: I need some air (*She walks out*)

Bishop Anders: Sally. I'm sorry

Sally: No you are not. If I had not caught you it would have continued Trent.

Bishop Anders: I love her Sally but I love you more

Sally: Noooooooo (*Crying out loud*). You love no one Trent. I'm not a kid anymore. I don't want anything to do with you anymore. The only reason I'm staying is for my grandkids. I promised their father I will take care of them so you pack your things and go to your lover's house okay? Go Trent. I loved you from my heart Trent and I always will but leave please.

Bishop Anders: I will leave. My brother Troy will come pick my things.

Sally: (*Leaving the lounge*) they will be in the garage. I don't want to see his face either. God will reward both of you accordingly and your mum who gave you this ill vice. (*Joey meets Sally on his way in*) He is in the lounge. Don't kill him

Joey: Thank you ma'am.

Bishop Anders: it's out son

Joey: Mum told me. What are you going to do?

Bishop Anders: I'm going to your mothers. April went out. Act like you didn't know as well otherwise you will be joining me.

Joey: No problem. Will see you later sir

Chapter Seven

Keith: Dad you will never believe whom I saw two days ago

Kathleen: He hasn't stopped talking about him at home. We had to ban his name on the table

Keith: Which is not fair by the way. It's Josh (*Abel stops what he is doing and looks at Keith*)

Abel: where is he? I have been looking for him.

Keith: Something going on dad?

Tina: your father has been dreaming about Josh a lot lately. He has to talk to him

Keith: I gave him my card. He will call. He wasn't looking well though. He's been on the streets for a while I could tell. He looked rough. I tried to make him come home with me but you know Josh, he believes in giving not receiving.

Abel: A lot has happened to him son. He was adopted by the rich man who killed his parents but he didn't remember the accident. The man loved him but not the wife so when the man died, he left his wealth to Josh but as you said Josh is Josh, he gave it to the man's wife. She fired him and he left the house. He had a fiancé but they fought and he just left. Two beautiful kids

Keith: A boy and a girl he told me. Why didn't you tell me maybe I could have convinced him?

Abel: Some things we leave for God son and at the same time it's Josh. How is Aunt Helen doing Kathleen?

Kathleen: she is fine. She got the kids for the weekend

Tina: Will she be able to run around with them energetic little ones?

Keith: Surprisingly they are calm and clingy when they are with her, no running around. She says we are the ones who do not know good parenting. I will take that for two days without them

Tina: Men

Keith: Mum, you too say that?

Tina: am I not allowed to say that. Remember I was a young woman once (*They all laugh*)

Rose: Are you going to call?

Joshua: sorry?

Rose: You have been looking at that card for the past two days

Joshua: I don't know. We used to be the best of friends you know. When we sang it was the most beautiful feeling and joy we ever felt in our lives. For me it was all about perfection because I believed God was perfect . . . (***Rose interrupts***)

Rose: and He still and will always be perfect. Son one man who will ever be perfect is Jesus and He is God Himself. Don't ever forget that. Why did you stop singing?

Joshua: One day Victoria caught me worshipping and told me God would never listen because I was never good enough.

Rose: Oh no; son that was the devil speaking. He knew if he stops you then he will entrap you. If you are finding it hard to read His word; start by worshipping and prayer. It was not by chance you met your best friend son. God send you someone you always cared for to help you get on your feet. I believe these few days we are sleeping in this small motel it's your friend?

Joshua: I saw you trembling the other night so I thought we could do with some new and warm clothes, a nice hot bath and a good bed.

Rose: How long are we staying here then?

Joshua: I had booked one night so we could have a good bath before we put new clothes on but the manager said once a year they do some offers so we can stay here for the next 5 weeks for free.

Rose: That's what God does son. Search Him you are not far off from discovering Him. In this life you sow seeds and reap them. All your life you have given whole heartedly and now you are reaping the fruits of your labour son. Any mother would be proud to call you her son. (*Tears fall from his eyes*) it's going to be okay. God loves you and everything happens for a reason.

Joshua: But how do I pray? How do I understand what His word says? How do I trust in His messages?

Rose: I do not have the entire answers son but one thing I know is that when God gives a promise and an oath it becomes unchangeable because He never lies. I gave you the bible, read yourself *Hebrew 6 verses 18-19.* Get me some food before you read your bible

Joshua leaves to get some food, when he returns after a few minutes he finds Rose unresponsive and quickly calls for an ambulance. They take Rose and Joshua to the hospital and straight to the emergency room as Josh waits in the waiting room alone pacing about.

Joshua: God I don't know if you can hear me now but I need you. She is all I got. I know I have misplaced my priorities but I promise I will do whatever you want if you bring her back to me. Lord all I can do is hope and I pray it is enough. Please God, don't take her away from me (*Kneeling down in tears*). I am sorry God but she doesn't deserve this. She has been suffering all her life. I will take care of her with your help if you let me. Please . . . . (*There is a knock on the door*)

Doctor: Excuse me sir

Joshua: Joshua Jones

Doctor: Yes Mr Jones. Is that your mother?

Joshua: No. I met her on the streets and started taking care of her so she is just like my mum to me. I'm all she has got and she is all I got.

Doctor: Okay sir, well she has got blood in her brain and right now they have taken her to surgery. The doctors will do the best they can but we just wanted to make sure she doesn't have insurance and the bills?

Joshua: it's alright Doctor. We will pay. Do what you have to do and I will get you the money. Just keep her alive. (*As he takes out his hand to shake the doctor's hand, Keith's card falls off his pocket*) thank you doctor.

Doctor: will let you know of the progress (*Doctor Leaves*)

Joshua: I will be damned. (*He goes to the nurses' station and asks to use the phone*). Please can I use your phone? I need to call family regarding my mum

Nurse: No problem.

Joshua: Thank you. (*He calls Keith and Keith answers*)

Keith: Hello

Joshua: it's Josh. I need your help; I am at the hospital St Rivers Hospital.

Keith: I am coming right away. (*He hangs up*) Dad let's go.

Tina: what's going on?

Keith: Josh needs my help. He is at St Rivers' Hospital.

Tina: we are all going. I will get the coats. Kathleen help me dear.

Abel: is he the one in trouble?

Keith: I don't know dad and I don't care. If Josh needs help its extremely serious

Abel: I believe that. *(**He puts on his shoes**)*

BISHOP ANDERS' CHURCH

Woman 1: I do not think it is appropriate for Sally to sit in front next to Connie.

Woman 2: Who is Connie again?

Woman 1: Joey's mum. You know Joey the youth leader right?

Woman 2: Oh yes I do. Why not? She is the worship leader and the Bishop's wife what is wrong with that?

Woman 1: Didn't you hear?

Woman 2: What did I miss?

Woman 1: Oh dear, you really are behind with the latest. Bishop Anders has been having an affair for 15 years with Connie and he is little Loraine's dad.

Woman 2: How did I miss this hot topic? So is he still with Sally then?

Woman 1: He chose Connie so he moved out.

Woman 2: Sally had it coming. She was trying to be all perfect at those women's meetings telling us to love our husbands alone yet hers is in the sack with the worship leader. You had about Victoria right?

Woman 1: Oh yes I did. That one is a devil in sheep skin. She had a perfect man but she chose the younger brother to have kids with

Woman 2: (*Laughing*) I would choose the younger brother as well. He is good looking and all manly. I need to come to church every Sunday just in case there is latest.

Woman 1: Let's wait and see what Anders has to say for himself. (*They both look up as the announcements finish and Bishop Anders walks up to the podium*)

Bishop Anders: Thank you all for attending this celebration at the start of your weekend. I know it was meant to be mine and Sally's 25th anniversary celebration but I am sorry to say we are no longer together. It was under mutual consent that we have both left this marriage. Please understand that it was a difficult decision for both of us but we would like to thank you for doing this for us and your support. I hope you all enjoy this celebration. Thank you. (*He leaves the stage*)

April: Mum you okay?

Sally: I will be fine darling. No man can keep me down. I'm going to go home now. I will take the kids.

April: I will come with you.

Sally: No darling. Stay and give a hand where it is needed. It's Friday after all. Have some fun.

April: (*Hugs Sally*) Call me if you need anything mum. I will come quickly. (*Sally leaves*)

Keith: I came here as soon as you called. How is she?

Joshua: Nothing yet *(He looks at Abel)* Sir we meet again. I wanted to call but . . . .

Abel: (*He hugs him*) No need to explain son. When it's time with God it will happen as it is meant to. How you holding up?

Joshua: Alright I guess.

Tina: Oh dear! Give me a hug. You have grown (*She hugs him).* You remember Kathleen right?

Joshua: Aunt Helen's niece. I do remember her.

Keith: She is family now

Joshua: Your wife you mean.

Keith: Of course . . . *(Doctor enters)*

Doctor: Sorry to interrupt. Didn't expect to see lots of people and I believe you are the sister *(Pointing to Tina)*

Tina: Excuse me?

Doctor: You look a lot like our patient so I assumed. I'm sorry. Anyway the surgery went well and she is in recovery but I will let you know when you can see her. I will take my leave. *(He leaves)*

Tina: Sorry son to ask you this. Who is the patient?

Joshua: About a month after I was on the street, I met this old lady and I started taking care of her. I would go and look for food, blankets and all sorts you would need and in return she kept telling me about God. She has been on the streets for 15 years and she has no family. Her husband was a . . . . *(Tina interrupts)*

Tina: A Bishop. Her name is Rose. She has a daughter but estranged because of the husband. *(She starts crying and Keith embraces her)*

Abel: It's her sister.

Joshua: She didn't mention anything about a sister

Abel: She wouldn't son. She blamed herself for the broken relationship. It was after their parents' death; Tina was young and a bit wild and Rose tried acting like her mum to protect her but Tina told her she needed a sister not a mum. The last straw was when Rose's boyfriend and later husband Troy tried to rape her and they had a confrontation both of them

forcing Rose to choose but she couldn't and Tina ran away.
A few years later Tina had found the Lord and went back to
find her sister only to discover nobody knew where she was
and she discovered she had a niece but the niece hated Rose
for trying to ruin her life for saying she was her mum.

Joshua: She told me about her daughter and husband and all but
not about her sister. She is the only one who loves me despite
all my weaknesses and she never hid her feelings from me. She
is the mum I never had. We were in the motel and talking
about calling Keith. She asked me to get her some food when
I returned she was unresponsive and I brought her here. The
doctor told me she had blood in her brain and it would cost
load. I told them to do the operation and called Keith straight
away.

Abel: and you have done the right thing son. You brought my
wife to her sister and I could not ask more from you son. You
are family and always will be. I dreamt of you before Peter
passed on. You were troubled and blaming yourself for your
father's death but God send me to you son. It was not your
fault and neither was Peter's. God never left you and He is
waiting for you to talk to Him. He loves you so much He has
a bigger plan for your life. He knows all your faults and He
has forgiven you already. You had a passion for worship son
and I think you need to start from there if everything else
doesn't make sense. Seek Him in your singing. I'm here, Keith
is here and so is God. We are going to help you stand again
son (***He embraces Josh***). God loves you we are going to get
through this together. Thank you for bringing Rose home.
(***Nurse enters***)

Nurse: You can go and see her now

Abel: You go first Josh. I think she wants to see you more than us (*Josh follows the nurse and sits next to Rose and takes her hand in his)*

Joshua: I know you can hear me Mama. You will be happy to know I prayed to God when I brought you here. I didn't know what else to do. I just said whatever I felt in my heart and it felt right and I also called Keith after I finished praying. His card fell out of my pocket and as you would say God told me to call him and for sure He did because I found out Keith is your nephew. Your sister Tina is his mom. She is here crying because she is sorry Mama. You never told me about her but you had your reasons. Her husband is a good man of God. She is alive and happy (*Rose opens her eyes and Josh stands up).* Mama Rose, I knew you heard me. Don't say anything I am going to get your sister and she looks a like you. (*Tears fall off her eyes)* as you would say, it's okay to cry especially when God's presence is around. I was listening you see? (*He smiles and leaves the room)*

IN THE WAITING ROOM . . . .

Abel: (*Holding Tina)* God works in mysterious ways for sure.

Keith: I know right. Meeting Josh again gave me an aunt I never knew. This is quite some family reunion. It feels good though you know. It's just an exciting inexplicable feeling. (*Josh enters)*

Joshua: We can all go see her now.

Victoria: You need to help me find Josh

Chad: Why now mum? I thought he was a worthless orphan whom no one loved.

Victoria: I was wrong.

Drew: No the clients won't sign deals without Joshua. (***Victoria keeps silent***) I knew it.

Victoria: I am your mother for Christ sake. You do not talk like that

Chad: That ship sailed a long time ago mum. When we tried looking for Josh you had a go at us. He was a good brother. The best we could ever ask for. Even though you didn't want anything to do with him, we went to see his kids because he asked us to. He said he will come back and see us when he is ready so we waiting for him mum. Unlike you, Josh keeps his promises so we are not going to make an effort in looking for him.

Victoria: Do you know if we don't get these deals we could be homeless within three months

Drew: We don't care mum. It's your wealth.

Victoria: (***Walking out of the room***) I sure did not birth you two

Drew: You did mum but we didn't agree with your character so we adopted dad's.

Russell: Boys what's going on with your mum?

Chad: She wants us to help her look for Josh otherwise we will be homeless in three months

Russell: Are you going to?

Drew: No dad. He will come back when he is ready you said so yourself and mum needs a lesson. She can't have everything she wants by ill-treating people. She needs to change her heart.

Russell: Only God can change one's heart boys. Your mum deserves forgiveness and another chance.

Chad: We know but she needs to suffer a bit and she will appreciate everyone even you. She feels superior and untouchable and the only way she will learn is if she falls first.

Russell: Are you sure you boys are 19? You are talking like grown-ups now.

Drew: Living with mum made us this. No disrespect but mum's hunger for power makes her act like a child sometimes leaving us to grow up quickly.

Russell: (*Laughing and leaving the room*) Okay boys let me see how she is coping.

Chad: You think we are being mean?

Drew: We are mum's sons after all (*They laugh and continue playing*)

Chapter Eight

Tina: I'm off to the hospital. I have left some food in the warmer

Abel: Okay dear will see you later. (***Tina leaves***) What has been troubling you son?

Joshua: Nothing sir

Abel: There is always something. I'm listening

Joshua: I miss my kids a lot. I haven't seen them in almost 5 months but if I go it means I got to see April

Abel: Is that a bad thing?

Joshua: I found her in bed with someone else. You tell me what do I get to say to her?

Abel: Son that was wrong what she did but you love her right?

Joshua: I don't know sir

Abel: Love has no switch, its either you love her or not. When you first met her and got to know her, how did you feel?

Joshua: I felt I could conquer the world. I felt like as long as I am with her nothing else will ever matter. I feel I cannot love any other woman except her. When we looked at each other we just knew we were meant to be. We could feel each other's pain.

Abel: Then go son and tell her that. Go and tell her that no matter what the devil tried to do your love for each other is stronger than his schemes. *(There is a rapid knock on the door)* I will go and see who it is? *(He goes to the door and finds Drew standing there)* Son????????

Drew: Sir I didn't know how to get hold of Josh; I thought you might have heard anything so I drove as quickly as I could. I just hoped you hadn't moved because its his son?

Joshua: What happened to Jojo? *(Drew just hugs Josh and won't let go)* Drew talk to me *(He looks at Drew's busted lip)* what happened?

Drew: I had a fight with Joey. Jojo is in hospital. Joey pushed him down the stairs and he was unconscious when they took him to the hospital. Mrs Anders called home so we went to the hospital that's where I had a scuffle with Joey. Chad is with dad, April and Mrs Anders at the hospital.

Joshua: Let's go. Give me the keys Drew

Abel: Son you can't drive in that state.

Joshua: I can and I will sir. If you not coming with me you bring Drew because nothing is stopping me from driving.

Abel: I will come with you but I am driving; if I have to beat you up to get those keys I will and I believe you know I can do that (***Josh gives him the keys***). That's what I thought

----

Russell: Calm down son

Chad: No dad. Wait till we find Josh. He will bust you up

Joey: Young man I am sorry. It was an accident and I should not have quarrelled with him but could you stop with those threats because I will bust you up like your twin and that Josh of yours as well. I am sorry okay. I was angry and I didn't mean for it to occur.

Sally: Please lets all calm down. Fighting won't resolve anything. (***Karen starts crying***) now you are making the baby cry.

Chad: I will take her out so that I don't get to face this crazy man before I rearrange his ugly face (***He takes Karen out and Russell laughs***)

Russell: Young people

Sally: I know. Have you managed to find Josh?

Russell: Nothing at all. I'm praying for him. He has been wronged so many times he just need time to recover and find his feet again.

Sally: I know. I just wish he knows his son is in hospital, he might come back. Maybe its all in God's plans. (***Bishop Anders arrives with Joey's mum and Troy***)

Bishop Anders: April honey, I came as soon as your mum called.

Sally: She hasn't said a word since we came. She's been crying and quiet about all this.

Troy: Hello Sally

Sally: Troy

Troy: it's been long

Sally: Has it? Haven't noticed. I thought you would come alone since this only involves family Trent?

Troy: Oh we are family Sally

Sally: I don't remember you sending anything to raise these kids Trent.

Troy: Still a bitter Sally I have always known . . . *(Josh enters the room and launches himself unto Joey they scuffle until Russell holds Josh off)*

Joey: Bring it. Let him go

Joshua: Let me go uncle Rus. I will destroy him.

Russell: He is not worth it son. The most important person is lying in that emergency room.

Abel: He is right Josh. You are better than that.

Joshua: it's my son. He is only six years old. How could he do that?

Sally: I know son but fighting won't undo what has already happened.

Troy: He is feisty as you said Trent

Russell: What did you say? (*Russell let go of Joey and punches Troy. Fighting enhances, Josh and Joey, Troy and Russell. Connie and Sally start exchanging words. The whole room is chaotic. No one can control anyone. Abel and Trent are trying to hold off the men then Tina walks in with Rose on a wheelchair and shouts*)

Tina: STOP! Aren't you all ashamed? (**They all start sitting down**) grown man. Bishops in the house of the Lord are fighting in the hospital. What kind of people are you?

Joey: He started it (*Pointing at Joshua*)

Tina: I do not care who started it. It has to stop. My husband sends me a text that Josh's son is in the emergency room. I brought my sister her because a little innocent boy's life is in the balance and what do I find?

Rose: Troy Anders.

Troy: Rose

Joshua: thanks uncle Rus for beating him, he deserves it more.

Rose: he does deserve it but God is the one who punishes him not us. Why are you fighting?

Joshua: Mama he pushed my boy down the stairs

Joey: It was an accident

Rose: Josh, what got into you son? Do you even hear yourself? Pointing fingers at each other like little boys. That's not the Josh who brought me here and looked after me in the streets.

Joshua: I'm sorry. I just felt so angry I wanted to beat him up. I was planning to go and see my boy today then Drew came to say Jojo was in hospital and he had a busted lip from Joey. All the way here I saw Joey's face. I wanted to kill him. I'm sorry ma'am.

Rose: Young man (*looking at Joey*) what have you got to say for yourself?

Joey: I found Jojo playing with an electric shaver. I told him it was dangerous and he shouldn't play with it. He started screaming at me telling me to leave the house because I am not his dad and all. He started kicking me and I just nudged him telling him to stop it but he lost his balance and fell down the stairs and I called the ambulance straight away. I didn't mean to hurt him. It was an accident. I'm sorry.

Rose: You need to put your differences aside and be here for that boy. He needs prayers not his dad and grandpas fighting. (*Tina seats next to Sally with Rose's wheelchair next to April and there is silence in the room until Karen makes baby sounds*)

Karen: Dada, dada (*Josh takes her from Chad*)

Joshua: Yes daddy's little princess. Let's see nana (*He takes her to Rose as people start conversing in the room*) this is little Karen.

Rose: Such an angel like daddy. (*She laughs*) and the smile as well

Troy: Rose can we talk?

Joshua: (*Standing up to face Troy*) I think your time to talk elapsed 15years ago. You never deserved her and because of her I will be civil to you but you deserve every punch that lands on your face. You do not even deserve any woman. Any man who proclaims to be a man of God and commits adultery leaving his wife who stood by him and never gave up on him when everybody laughed at him is just like any stone trying to float on water when it knows it is going to sink. You see this woman sat in this wheelchair has loved me more than any other woman who has been in my life. She has believed in me more than anyone has in my entire life and all I want is to hate you but I do not have space for you because it is occupied by love. When you face God and He asks you what you did with the gift He gave you, I do not know what answer you will present to Him. One thing I have learnt is I wasted too much time trying to make your brother and Victoria love me, I forgot God loves me and man can hate me but He never will hate me even if I do wrong. So I will ask you politely for you and your brother's entourage to leave. This is my son so I do have the right to who needs to be here and Bishop Trent Anders, I do not hold anything against you but Sally is the greatest thing that could ever have happened to you because none of us would have been here if she hadn't given birth to your daughter. Don't be surprised, Drew told me on our way here that you left Sally for Joey's mum but nothing surprise me because it looks like it runs in the family. Now if all of you would leave. (***Trent, Troy, Joey's mum and Joey start walking out***)

Joey: April let's go

Drew: (*Laughing*) don't be so daft; her son is in hospital where do you think she is going. Maybe Josh knocked his brain out. (*Chad, Russell and Abel laugh as well*)

Sally: Thank you Josh. (*Doctor walks in*)

Doctor: Sorry for the long wait we needed to be certain. I need the parents. (*Josh and April stand next to each other*) Mr Jones

Joshua: Yes Doctor, it's my son. What's wrong?

Doctor: The good news is he just broke his arm only but the bad news is he suffered some bleeding in the brain and we won't know until the surgery is done if he suffered any brain damage. I'm sorry Mr Jones but this time it's a 50/50 chance.

Joshua: Thank you doctor. Do what you have to. He is a strong boy he will pull through. (*He shakes the doctor's hand and the doctor leaves. April starts crying more and Sally makes her sit down and embraces her whilst Josh paces around scratching his head*)

Rose: You need to sit down son.

Joshua: I'm alright. He is going to be fine right Mama?

Rose: Yes he is but you need to be alright for him. If he is like you he will pull through quickly.

Abel: Listen to Rose son. God is going to take care of him.

Joshua: Yeah I guess so but I feel hot. I need some air.

Drew: But it's cold out there

Russell: No I need some air as well

Abel: Me too (*all the men go out*)

Sally: I'm sorry Rose; I wish I had done something back then

Rose: You wouldn't have succeeded my dear but it's okay. You know the Anders boys, hardened boys. I wish I had known Josh meant your daughter when he told me about her. I would have knocked him with a brick (*They laugh*)

Sally: it's alright. He was hurt by those he loved the most it's understandable. He is a good boy

Rose: I know. Because of him I got my sister back. The streets were not a good place but he made sure I ate three times a day even if he didn't have anything. He got some old blankets and all these things. How he got all the things I failed to get for 15 years in the streets I do not know. April honey look up here. (*April wipes her tears and looks at Rose*) How do you feel about all this? I can see you have not said a word since all this.

April: (*Crying*) all I wanted was for my son to have a dad to play with every time. I didn't know it would cost him his life

Rose: No dear he will not lose his life. We serve a mighty God and He will see us through. I do not know how you feel about that young man who left with your father but what I know is my Joshua loves you so much that he does not know what to do when you are crying like this. He won't say a word because he needs a smack sometimes but what I truly believe is if he can't have you he is going to give up on marriage. You need to talk to him.

April: but he won't even look at me

Rose: because he wants to be angry at you but he knows when he looks at you he will just want to love you and he sees it as a weakness which is good for us. We use it against him dear. Your boy is going to be okay but you two need to sort out your issues before you see that boy.

Outside . . . .

Russell: How are you?

Joshua: I don't really know. I just feel like everything is like a dream. You know before dad died, he told hope is will get me through it all. I wanted to believe it but I couldn't because what I felt that day still haunts me.

Abel: Have you sought help about it?

Joshua: I'm just an orphan and no medication can take this away.

Abel: because that's not the help you need. You need to admit it, to say it, to shout and release it then ask God to help you heal son. Medication never heals it only treats. Tell me how you feel now

Joshua: I feel lonely, confused. When I read the bible I get even more confused

Abel: and that is the right step. Only God can give revelation and you need to ask Him for it. All I can ever say to you is talk to Him. Act crazy if that's the way you can talk to Him. We are different at the end of the day so do what you got to do. What we man can only do is encourage nothing more.

Chad: Look who is here? (***Victoria walks towards them***)

Drew: Trouble in paradise

Russell: Hope you don't mind Josh. I told her you here

Joshua: No problem. I'm here for my son and it's his granny after all

Drew: I am kind of hungry

Abel: Will come with you. Might as well get the ladies something to eat

Russell: I will come as well (***They all leave Joshua standing by himself with Victoria approaching***)

Joshua: Victoria

Victoria: Hi Joshua. You look (***keeps quiet for a bit***) . . . . thin

Joshua: why thank you. Apparently being homeless don't give you the courtesy of a personal chef

Victoria: I see you have learnt to be sarcastic as well

Joshua: Oh believe me I learnt quite a lot of things. I can see you got a heart now. Visit my son in hospital

Victoria: Actually I came to see you. The Harrison Company is not renewing our contract unless you they negotiate with you. I only got a couple weeks left till they change suppliers. I need you to do this for me please otherwise I will lose everything

Joshua: (*Laughing sarcastically*) I can't believe you. Everything is about you Victoria. You do not even care about anyone else and here I thought you came to see my son. I am nothing remember. No one loves me. I don't care about that because at least I love my kids and I will do anything for them but you are just a selfish greedy mother who doesn't know how to appreciate others and what she has got. You always want more even though it's not yours. I tried so much to make you love me but you can't love. I'm sorry. I'm not a Jones by blood remember I am a charity case who got nothing but just to let you know, I am alright the way I am. Stay away from me please otherwise I will lose it (*He walks away*)

Victoria: (*Shouting after him*) I don't need you (*Josh looks back and smiles*)

Joshua: I never said you did. Bye Vicky

Rose: How have you been Sally?

Sally: What can I say?

Rose: Nothing I haven't experienced myself. At least you still got a house

Sally: Oh yes. I told him to leave and pay the bills otherwise he will meet my fist and kicks (*They all laugh*)

Rose: How I have missed your jokes. You seen my Wendy?

Sally: I did and I told her all about you. She wanted to throw tantrums but I made sure she heard what I wanted to say. When I left she was a bit disturbed but i told her all Rose because justice needs to be done.

Rose: aaaaaw Sally. Thank you

Sally: I thank God that He saved me because really I would have knocked so many people and Mrs Anders I told her a good piece of my mind.

Rose: Sally some things you just leave for God.

Sally: I know Rose but the words she said to me are the ones which made me react. I just told her the truth Rose (*Josh Enters*). Where are the men?

Joshua: Gone to get some lunch.

Rose: Sally and Tina why don't you take me out for some air.

Joshua: I will take you.

Rose: No you are staying with April. The doctor might return and want to see the parents. You are not going anywhere until everything is sorted especially between you two. You have two kids here and you don't talk to each other. It needs to stop. These kids deserve better than that. We will take Karen with us and you are not leaving this room. Am I clear?

Joshua: Yes ma'am.

Rose: At least we have an understanding

Sally: A forced one

Rose: If it works so be it.

Sally: I will push the wheelchair

Tina: (*taking Karen from April*) okay. (*They leave the room and there is complete silence between April and Josh till Josh speaks*)

Joshua: The first time I held your hand I knew I wasn't going to let you go. I knew that I was going to marry you no matter what. I felt so complete when you smiled at me or blushed. All that mattered to me was that you were happy. When I found you with Joey that day, I felt a shudder in my heart. I felt so hurt that I wanted to erase any memory of you and I wish it were that easy. I wasn't just angry at you or Victoria, I was angry at God as well but Rose told me off and I realised God is never responsible for man's wrong doings. You hurt me April and I pray for God to erase that day from my heart completely because it has become my weakness. I just wish we hadn't fought. I tried so hard those three weeks to come see you and the kids but Victoria made me work no matter how I tried to beg her. I tried explaining to you but you were so angry you never listened. I think we need to come to a mutual understanding now. Your mum told me you started university again so I will come get the kids for the whole week and you can have them over the weekend. I'm going to go (*He stands up and turns to leave*)

April: (*Crying*) Josh please! (*He looks back and sees her kneeling on the floor crying*) I tried so many times to undo that day Josh but I could not. Since that day I never consummated my relationship with Joey. Everyday just thinking what might have happened to you I couldn't cope. I forced myself to like Joey that I may forget you but it didn't work. I told myself so many times that you would never matter to me again but I was lying to myself. When you cried and said you never want to see me again I began hating myself and have never stopped. If I could turn back time I would Josh that I may not hurt you but listen to you. I can't change anything Josh but I can't go on knowing you don't want anything to do with me anymore. I love you so much Josh and I don't love anyone else so please just kill me now and save me from myself. I AM SO SORRY Josh. Please forgive me. (*She cries even more and Josh just looks at her shivering in her hurt and loneliness and kneels next to her and holds her face in his hands*)

Joshua: Look at me April. It's going to be alright. (*Tears in his eyes*) Our son is going to be fine and we will take him home. Please just don't cry like this. I love only you and nothing will ever change that. I just need to find my way and I forgive you with all my heart. (*He embraces her as she keeps crying*) everything is going to be okay. I know it will.

Chapter Nine

Rose: I am going to live with Sally

Tina: You can stay here as long as you want

Rose: I know dear but she needs somebody and I will be there for her. I know what she is going through and I can help her. I will be fine Tina. We will visit you every day or you can visit

Tina: Okay I guess. Just don't want to think I am losing you again

Rose: You never lost me. Josh won't leave the hospital until his son wakes up so Abel said he will take me

Tina: Make sure I see you

Victoria: (*With tears on her face*) Please Lawrence you cannot resign.

Lawrence: Just give me one good reason not to.

Victoria: My boys will lose what their father left for them. Our house is about to be repossessed and please. I wanted to have it all Lawrence but I can't and couldn't but my boys.

Lawrence: That's a good reason Vicky but I cannot. I got family to look after (*Joshua from behind*)

Joshua: and you still can

Lawrence: Josh????

Joshua: Hey Lawrence

Lawrence: How did you . . . .

Joshua: Uncle Russell. I was at the hospital with my son when he called. I didn't want to leave but he begged me because Victoria has been suffering apparently

Lawrence: But it's already late.

Joshua: No its not. I called Harrisons on my way here. I explained that my son is in the hospital so I couldn't make it so they agreed to meet me today here. Lawrence could you give us a minute please?

Lawrence: Sure Josh and I will take my letter with me. I am so happy to see you (*He leaves*)

Joshua: In the 21years I have lived with you I have never seen you cry Victoria. What happened?

Victoria: pride got hurt as it seems. Humiliation and embarrassment followed.

Joshua: Uncle Russell is a good man. He loves you truthfully

Victoria: I know (***Wiping tears away***). Can I ask you something?

Joshua: Of course

Victoria: When you heard me telling Peter that I would never love you, why did you keep on loving me?

Joshua: when you are a child you don't choose who to love. All you want is a mum and dad who loves you and embraces you when you have done wrong.

Victoria: *(Crying)* Why don't you hurt me or spite me?

Joshua: and gain what? You are my mum even the birth certificate says so even though my surname and biological parents' name got changed. Victoria sometimes in life those you hate or who hurt you the most are the ones you also love the most. Love is not a switch you can turn off any time you want. It does not go away because you are angry. The more you are angry the more the love grows. You will always be my mum and no matter what you did to me, I will always love you. The reason why I signed over the company is so that you discover there is more to life other than wealth Victoria. I hope you have learnt that. I got to go to my son now. He might be awake. (***He starts walking out and Victoria calls out***)

Victoria: Joshua, I'm sorry. I hope you forgive me. I don't deserve your love or gifts

Joshua: it's not me. It's God and we all don't deserve what we got but it's His grace that makes us worth it.

Victoria: (***Walking toward him***) If I could be your mum again son and I spoke to the lawyer, this is your and your brothers' company and you deserve it son. He will come tomorrow and sort it all out. (***She embraces him***) Thank you

Joshua: (***Smiling***) No mum thank you. You called me son and you have given me a mother's first hug after 21 years mum. I love you mum

Victoria: Love you too son. You go to the hospital; I will just clear the office for you and you find it ready when you come back. I will retire early and go love your uncle as he deserves.

Joshua: (***Laughing***) I think he will love it

----

1 MONTH LATER

AT CHURCH . . . .

Abel: The Lord has been great to me and my family. I just would like to take this opportunity to call upon Joshua Jones. Many of you remember him as a young boy who used to sing with my son in church. Now he is a handsome man and father and next week a husband. His testimony is one which many will look at and realise the great power of God's love and mercy. Son come and take it up (***Joshua goes on stage***)

Joshua: Amen

Congregation: Amen

Joshua: thank you people of God. The Lord has been amazing to me. A couple months ago I lost everything I had in 24 hours. I became homeless but as they say home is where the heart is I met the most amazing woman who reminded me that with God's presence and grace every painful situation is nothing but a drop in an ocean. This woman is Mama Rose and don't mess with her because you will answer to me. Through it all I have been reunited with my fiancé whom I love very much, my kids, my brothers and my mum. The last time I sang I was five so please forgive me if I am rusty. i kindly ask you all to join me as I begin to worship Him who has brought us all here today. April the one thing I never told you was I could sing so please don't make me sing to you as a punishment. (*Congregation laughs and the instruments start playing in the back ground*) This song is called reborn for a second chance. (*He starts singing*)

"Your favour has turned my life around
As I drowned in painful memories of my past
You rained you peace upon me
Man has stumbled on me
But you cleansed me in spiritual purity

CHORUS
My heart has been restored
My mind has been renewed
And my love for you is overwhelming
All I ever wanted was your friendship
But God you gave me more
A chance to be reborn in your presence

I shall delight in wisdom
I shall praise in humility
I shall tremble in your presence
And I shall die singing Hallelujah
For all I know is to worship you my Lord"

The congregation start clapping hands as some fall on their knees with tears falling down their eyes. There is a noise of encouragement as Josh sings his heart out with tears now falling from his eyes.

MEANWHILE . . . .

Bishop Anders: What is going on Troy?

Troy: Wendy has gone to see Rose. She said she doesn't care whether I rot in hell or not and a lot of the church members have left. I am in serious financial strain could you help me out?

Bishop Anders: I am in the same situation brother. I do not know what to do.

Troy: we could form an alliance and become one church and sell the other building. It will save us both and we get the money we need

Bishop Anders: I like that idea. I will get it done. We never lose man

Troy: Otherwise mum will do serious damage to us.

Rose: You can sing son

Joshua: Thanks Mama.

Drew: Josh mum has to go

Joshua: Give me a minute Mama. (*He goes to Victoria and a young lady walking with April approaches Rose and Sally*)

April: Aunty Rose. Someone wants to see you (*Rose looks at the young lady*)

Rose: Wendy!!!!!!!!!! (*She hugs her with tears in her eyes*)

Wendy: (**Crying**) I am sorry mum. I didn't know.

Rose: It's okay darling. Your father initiated it. All that matters is you are here (*Josh approaches*)

Joshua: Mama you are crying. Are you weak now?

Rose: I am happy son. My daughter has come to me.

Joshua: Either way you were going to meet her next weekend she is the maid of honour

Rose: Why didn't you tell me?

Joshua: It was a surprise. Come on we are going to mum's for Sunday dinner. I told her Wendy was coming so come on.

April: Where are the kids?

Joshua: they have gone with mum. Karen wouldn't let go of mum so she took both of them. (*They all start walking towards the car. Josh lags behind with Rose*)

Rose: You got something to say?

Joshua: Thank you God and thank you Mama.

Rose: You are most welcome son. It was hope that made me survive on those streets for all those years and that same hope has given you more than your family back. It has taken you back to where it all started; to God.

Joshua: (*Smiling*) and hope shall remain a part of me as long as I shall live.

THE END . . . .